This edition published by Parragon Books Ltd in 2017 and distributed by

Parragon Inc.
440 Park Avenue South, 13th Floor
New York, NY 10016
www.parragon.com

ISBN 978-1-4748-7417-5

Printed in China

The Kitten Sitters

Bath · New York · Cologne · Melbourne · Delhi
Hong Kong · Shenzhen · Singapore

"Guess what?"
Mickey Mouse called
his nephews Morty
and Ferdie out into the
garden. "Minnie is going
away. We're going to
look after her kitten!"
   Morty and Ferdie
grinned. A kitten.
How exciting!

Cluck, cluck, cluck! There was a sudden flapping and the sound of angry crowing. Two figures burst through a hole in the fence. One of them was Pluto. He was being chased across the lawn by … an angry rooster!

As they raced across the lawn, Minnie and Figaro turned up.
Minnie shook a finger at Mickey's dog. "Pluto, not again! You're
so naughty for chasing chickens."

Pluto hung his head in shame. Not because he'd been scolded.
After all, Minnie wasn't his owner. But because he'd had to run
away from a rooster!

"It's a good thing Figaro is staying with you," Minnie told Mickey as she climbed back into her car. "Maybe he can teach Pluto how to behave."

Mickey picked up Figaro and they waved goodbye to Minnie.

"Let's go," Mickey said, tickling the kitten under the chin. "We're going to have fun, aren't we?"

Minnie was hardly out of sight when Figaro jumped out of Mickey's arms, raced into the kitchen, and pounced on the table. Mickey ran after him, but he was too late. *Crash!* A jug of cream fell to the floor.

The kitten's pink tongue lapped up the cream. Pluto gave a warning growl. You didn't eat off the floor here!

Mickey took a deep breath and started cleaning up. "Take it easy," he told his dog. "Figaro is our guest."

When dinnertime arrived, Pluto ate all his food like
a good dog. But no matter how hard Mickey and his
nephews tried, they couldn't tempt Figaro to touch the
special food Minnie had left for him.

When they all went to bed, Figaro had a special
cushion on the floor to sleep on. But he didn't go near it.
Instead, he bounced onto Ferdie's bed, tickling his ears
with the tip of his tail. Then he ran out of the room and
headed back to the kitchen.

"Uncle Mickey!" called Morty from his bedroom.
"Did you remember to close the kitchen window?"

"Oh no!" Mickey scrambled out of bed and quickly
raced downstairs.

A cold breeze flapped the kitchen curtains. Figaro was
nowhere to be seen!

"Figaro!" Mickey and his nephews searched high and low, calling to the kitten. Upstairs, downstairs, behind chairs, under tables. They even inspected every bit of the yard, looking for kitten paw prints. Nothing!

"You two stay here," Mickey told his nephews. "Pluto!"
Four tired paws padded out of the house. Mickey smiled.
"Come on, boy. Let's find Minnie's kitten."
The two of them set off, searching for the missing cat.

Their first stop was Minnie's house. "Maybe Figaro made his way home." Mickey muttered. There was no sign of a little, black-and-white cat.

Mickey marched toward town. "Keep walking, Pluto. He can't have gone far."

Mickey and Pluto arrived at the edge of the park. It was dark and empty, but they found a police officer walking the paths.

"Have you seen a black-and-white kitten?" Mickey asked with a hopeful smile.

"I certainly have!" said the man. He jerked a thumb over his shoulder. "Teasing the ducks…."

"Thank you!" Mickey cried. He and Pluto raced to the duck
pond. Finally, they found … a trail of muddy footprints.

"They must belong to Figaro," Mickey gasped. "Let's
follow them."

With Pluto's nose to the ground, they traced the paw prints
all the way out of the park to Main Street. A dairy truck driver
stood in the street.

"Have you seen a little, black-and-white kitten?" Mickey asked for the second time that night.

"I have!" the driver cried. "He came running along and knocked over all my eggs."

Mickey groaned as he paid for the broken eggs.

"Where are you, Figaro?" he called into the night.

Mickey and Pluto spent all night searching the town.
There was no sign of the missing kitten. By the time they
returned home, the sun was starting to rise.

Mickey was still in his bathrobe when Minnie pulled up
in her car.

"Where's Figaro?" she asked, beaming.

No one said a word.

Her smile faded. "Oh no. Something has happened to him!
Can't I trust you boys to look after one sweet, little kitten?"

Before Mickey could answer…

Squawk! Cluck! Cluck!

He recognized those sounds! In a flurry of feathers, three hens leapt over the fence with Figaro hot on their tails.

"There's your sweet, little kitten!" Mickey said. "He ran away last night. He chased the ducks in the pond, and he broke the eggs in the dairy van. And now he's, he's…"

"Chasing chickens!" Minnie said.

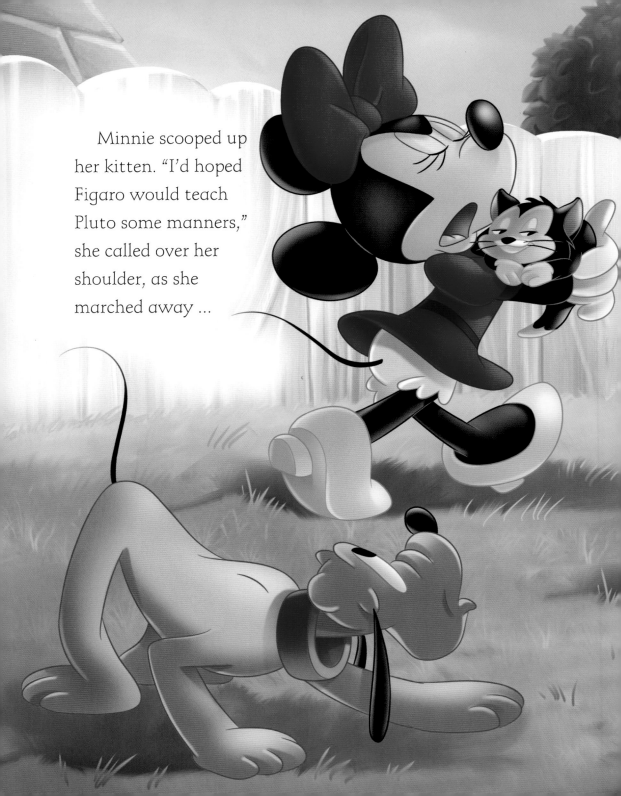

Minnie scooped up her kitten. "I'd hoped Figaro would teach Pluto some manners," she called over her shoulder, as she marched away ...

... "but your dog has shown my kitten how to be naughty!"

"Pluto didn't do anything wrong!" Ferdie said.

"It was Figaro!" added Morty.

Minnie wouldn't listen. She stomped off with Figaro grinning at them over her shoulder.

Minnie's car pulled away in a cloud of dust.

"Don't worry, boys," Mickey said. "We'll explain later on when she's calmed down."

Morty and Ferdie glanced at each other.

"You don't have to tell her right away, do you?" asked Morty. "As long as Aunt Minnie thinks Pluto is a bad dog, we won't have to kitten-sit Figaro."

Pluto's eyes lit up.

Mickey shrugged. "Maybe we should wait a while. We could all use some peace and quiet."

It had been a long night. He settled down on the grass, using Pluto's body as a pillow. Together, they fell asleep beneath the shade of a tree. There wasn't a kitten in sight. Which, for now, was just the way they liked it.